Give your child a head start with
PICTURE READERS

Dear Parent,

Now children as young as preschool age can have the fun and satisfaction of reading a book all on their own.

In every Picture Reader, there are simple words, rebus pictures, and 24 flash cards to cut out and keep. (There is a flash card for every rebus picture plus extra cards for reading practice.) After children listen to each story a couple of times, they will be ready to try it all by themselves.

Collect all the titles in our Picture Reader series. Once children have mastered these books, they can move on to Levels 1, 2, and 3 in our All Aboard Reading series.

ALL ABOARD READING™

A PICTURE READER

King Big Wig

By Portia Aborio
Illustrated by Sonja Lamut

Grosset & Dunlap • New York

Big Wig

was a .

He liked big things.

He liked his big

and his big 👑.

He liked his big

and his big  .

Every night,

the  gave him

a big  of  .

The liked that too.

One day,

the

was sailing

his toy  .

He got a big idea.

If big things are good,

bigger things are better!

So the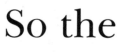

got a bigger

and a bigger .

He got a bigger

and a bigger .

But was the  happy?

No.

His was too big!

It fell in his 👁 👁

and it tickled his 👃.

Achoo!

His was too big!

It hurt his head.

"Ow!

I am going to  ,"

the said.

So off went the .

But he did not

find his .

His  was too big!

"Bigger is not better,"

the  said.

So what did

the  do?

He left his bigger  .

He got rid of

his bigger

and his bigger .

The  got

back his old

and his old

and his old .

Then the

got into his old .

But was the  happy?

Yes.

He was.

Until the  came in

with a bigger

of 🍨 .

Then the  was <u>very</u> happy!

"Sometimes bigger

is better," the  said.